I0539051

Also by Daniel Coshnear

Occupy & Other Love Stories (Kelly's Cove Press 2012)

"Years from now a Ph.D. student writing about the Occupy Movement will sure-ly point to *Occupy & Other Love Stories* an example of the fiction that emerged from the protests against Wall Street immorality and criminality. It's also fiction that stands on its own merits…Coshnear's stories are compact with vivid de-scriptions of people and places, and with crisp dialogue that's practically audi-ble." —Jonah Raskin, from *The Rag Blog*

"Chekhov, Joyce, Borges, William Trevor, Grace Paley, Alice Munro all give us epiphanies, fleeting wonders of life as in no other form but poetry…I think Dan Coshnear's book has that unity, that every story in *Occupy & Other Love Stories* is held together by a diffused, long sigh of regret for dreams lost or deferred, much like last year's Occupy Movement the title story and collection is named for." —Barbara Baer, *The Redwood Coast Review*

Jobs & Other Preoccupations (Helicon Nine 2001)

"Daniel Coshnear writes about a dozen kinds of desperation and a few kinds of peace with a mordant wit and the kind of emotional exactitude that clears a reader's vision the way a sharp new flavor clears and challenges the palate. He is a thrilling discovery." —Rosellen Brown

Homesick Redux

by Daniel Coshnear

Winner of the Fiction Fix Novella Award

Guest Editor: Raleigh Rand

Homesick Redux

© 2015 Daniel Coshnear. All rights reserved.
ISBN 978-0-578-16489-2
Typesetting and design by April Gray Wilder

Edited by Raleigh Rand

Editor-in-Chief	April Gray Wilder
Managing Editor	Alex Pucher
Associate Editor	Blair Romain
Asst. Managing Editor	Kelsi Hasden
Copyeditor	Sarah Cotchaleovitch
Editors Emeriti	Sarah Cotchaleovitch
	Melissa Milburn
	Thelma Young
Editorial Assistants	Sarah Cotchaleovitch
	Kristen Pickrell
	Kelsie Sandage
	Alex Cendrowski

Readers

Amanda Bova, Lindsay Chapman, Brandi Gaspard, Ali Huffman, Emily Michael, Jacqueline Partridge, Becky Pearson, Lori Selfick, Hurley Winkler

Fiction Fix is grateful for the support of the University of North Florida's Department of English.

Fiction Fix

www.fictionfix.net
editor@fictionfix.net

Thanks to my family, Susan, Circe and Daedalus, and my family, Dad, Rick, Val and Meem, for their support either in the creation of the story or in living through the real events upon which it is based. And thanks to my writer friends, David Porter, Harry and Linda Reid, Mike Tuggle, for blurbs and honest impressions and so many kindnesses. And thanks to the editors at *Fiction Fix* and Raleigh Rand. It's not easy to find a home for a long story – I'm grateful for their novella series. And finally, thanks to my dear mother without whom homesickness would not have been possible.

Homesick Redux

New York City, Winter 1986 –

He repeats the word *delisandwich* four times as we rise from the subway into pounding rain at Union Square.

"Come on, Milton," I say. "Walk faster. Five blocks to go."

Once, not long ago, I was so in love, we were having sex, Pia and I, and I had to fight the urge to scream, "Marry me! Marry me! Marry me!" I'm glad now I didn't say it. It would have been a disaster for both of us. I'm fighting the urge to say, "Milton, stop being so retarded." I said it once before, only once, and the poor man, you could see him go inside himself.

"Go on, then, walk slower. Let's get soaked." I shake and see beads of water fly from my nose and ears. It's a good feeling except for the t-shirt that's heavy and cold on my belly. "Come on, Milton." I jump off the curb into fifteen inches of raging river.

"I think you're nuts, mister."

"What do you want for lunch?"

"*Delisandwich.*"

"What kind?"

"You'll see," he says. And then, "You're crazy, mister." He needs windshield wipers for his aquarium-thick glasses. He stops to raise his dripping finger to the side of his head, and with a few slow rotations illustrates crazy. Blinking man turns to orange hand. I feel a fever coming on.

We arrive at the deli on Fifth Avenue, wet newspaper on the floor in the doorway, a bustle at the counter.

"You should've brought an umbrella," Milton says.

"*You* should've brought an umbrella."

I walk past two rows of booths to the bathroom in the back. When I return, Milton has neither found a seat nor stepped up to the counter. He's a small boulder in a stream of hungry customers. "Mr. Mittelman." I take his arm. "What would you ever do without me?" I don't expect an answer, except perhaps the rotating finger again.

He says, "I don't know, Reggie."

I'm stunned. And moved. I've been his bench-work supervisor for three years, and I've never heard him say my name. I guide him toward the back where I see a free booth. It's warm away from the door, and I'm enjoying the aroma of matzo ball soup, potato latkes, the rich mix of smells rising from the steam table, even the tang of ammonia. The warmth, the aromas, sudden respite from the masses, a shiver, fever coming on; I feel an inexplicable sadness, a swell of homesickness.

Trenton, NJ, Summer 1973 –

I'm from Baltimore, now visiting my uncle and some brand new cousins in a suburb of New Jersey. Uncle Jim has recently married a divorced woman, Jan, and she has two children, Michael, thirteen, and Stacy, sixteen. I'm eleven. This is my first time away from my immediate family, and the plan – not mine – is for a two-week visit. It is expected that Michael and I will become fast friends.

Uncle Jim drives me from the train station to the front of the house, brick bottom, aluminum siding above, like every other home for miles. Over a small cement front porch rests a white awning with a single green stripe – how I will recognize the house if I get lost. Uncle Jim is my least favorite uncle. Not because I know him or any of my mother's brothers well but because he is the bald one, and he has an embarrassing twitch, as if out of the blue he must bite the end off an invisible loaf of French bread. He seems to regard me as a little adult. His only words on the drive: "Racetrack is over that way." I see nothing but a chain-linked fence.

Michael is mowing the grass on the side of the lawn. He sees us but doesn't stop until Uncle Jim waves him in our direction. He still doesn't cut off the mower.

"This is your cousin, Reggie," says Uncle Jim with a bite.

Michael regards my corduroys, which are brand new, too large, and unevenly cuffed. "Hey."

"Why don't you show him those rabbits you found," says Uncle Jim.

"Bunnies," says Michael. "But they're dying. I have to drown them."

Uncle Jim makes no visible response. Did he hear what Michael just said? Aunt Jan comes down the front steps to greet me. I try not to stare at her bouncing white tank top.

"Hi, sweetie," she says. She's from Dallas, and so hers must be a Texas accent, but she sounds to me like our neighbor from Virginia. (About the neighbor: she had what was called a "nervous breakdown," and I saw her scratch another neighbor's face with her fingernails.) Jan cups my face in her hands. I am an inch from her breasts, some freckles descending in a dark crevice, and the feelings I'm having are new and painful. I'm shy. I know most people can read my mind. I turn my head out of Aunt Jan's grasp, and over her shoulder I see Cousin Stacy wearing short shorts, a halter top, and a vague sneer. "Stacy and I are going shopping," Aunt Jan tells Uncle Jim. "Michael, why don't you show Reggie your rabbits?"

"Bunnies," he says.

I follow Michael into the garage, my heavy suitcase clapping against my ankle. The two brown bunnies are curled in a cardboard box with a screen on top. Michael lifts the screen and grabs one by the loose fur of its neck. "I hit the mother with the lawn mower," he explains. "She must've been sick because she didn't get out of the way."

"You saw her?"

"Not really." He shrugs.

"How'd you get these guys?"

"They were under her." He holds the bunny close to a bare light bulb. "Look. It's got maggots." Maybe I can see something moving in its fuzzy ear. Maybe not. "Want to help me?"

"Drown them?"

"It's the best way." He hands me the quivering thing, smaller than one of those hamburgers you buy by the dozen. "I'll fill up the sink. You can do one and I'll do one."

"No thanks."

"You don't want to help me?"

"Well…"

"Never mind," he says. "Randy's coming over. He'll help me." He puts the bunny back in the box and leads me to his room. I heave my suitcase onto a bed. From Michael's window, I see Uncle Jim driving away. I assume we'll go find some of Michael's friends to play football, softball, kick-the-can, something – the stuff I'd have been doing at home. It's summer; maybe we'll go to a park and bring a Frisbee or go to a creek and look for turtles. Michael shows me his electric guitar and wa-wa pedal. On the record player he spins his favorite cut from the Woodstock album – Country Joe singing "The Fish Cheer." He sets the speakers in his bedroom window facing the street and waits for someone to pass, then blasts, "Give me an F! Give me a U! Give me a C!" We're shouting "FUCK" to the passing world. I think I can see why this would be fun, but very few people pass, and their responses are fairly dull and predictable. An elderly man with a quad cane turns his face halfway toward the house, grimaces as if he smells a dirty diaper, and hobbles on. Next, a black woman in a nurse's uniform wrinkles her nose. When Randy hears the story, however, he's impressed. He buckles in half on the front lawn.

"You're a crazy son of a bitch. You are one crazy motherfucker."

At eleven, I've had very little exposure to the world outside my neighborhood. Most of my guesses about people seem to be wrong. Somehow though, I guess that Michael will delight at the names Randy gives him. Michael buckles in half as Randy did. "You should've seen this fucking old man," he says. He looks at me for support, embellishment. He looks back at Randy, "And this crazy black nurse bitch."

"Hey, is this your cousin?" Randy gives me a thumbs-up handshake, which of course, I get wrong on the first try. "Cool," he says.

"He doesn't want to do the deed with the bunnies, man," Michael says. "But hey, that's cool."

"Yeah, we'll do it," says Randy.

"You can do whatever you want," Michael says. "You probably don't want to watch."

I'm a little impressed by Michael's sensitivity on this point. He seems conscious of my uneasiness, that I'm in a new setting and all. I wonder how long that will last. I sit on the front stoop and pretend to study the cover of the *Hardy Boys* adventure in my hand. Before the boys have turned the corner around the side of the house, I hear Michael say to Randy, "Two weeks, man."

And Randy, whose voice is louder, "Seems like a pussy."

Dinner is stewed tomatoes, rectangular slices of ham, creamed corn. We'd never eat that kind of thing at our house. The pink fluid from the tomatoes runs like a river across my plate. At home I can have separate bowls if I want. At home I can say no.

It's bedtime and Michael is organizing his drawers with a sense of urgency and secrecy. After a few minutes, he pulls out a shoe box with pins and stickers and an unusual-looking little pipe. He puts the pipe to his lips and pretends to inhale. He grins. I don't get it.

"Drugs are dangerous," he says.

"Yeah, I guess."

"Shit, look what happened to Hendrix."

"What?"

"You don't know what happened to Hendrix?"

I don't. I don't know who Hendrix is. And I don't know what happened to Michael's father. There's plenty I don't know, but I'm beginning to discover that being with my new cousin makes my stomach tense.

"Hendrix o-deed, man. Choked on his own vomit."

"What is o-deed?"

"Overdosed. Christ. He was flying on all kinds of shit. He started puking, and some stupid-ass nurse made him hold his head up. That was it."

"Huh."

"And it was the same shit with Joplin."

"She took too many drugs, too?"

"Choked on her own puke."

The following day, I tag along as Michael and Randy collect two other friends to plan a night of camping out. Presumably, the plan has been approved by Aunt Jan or Uncle Jim, though neither ever seem to be around. Planning and planning – a real conspiracy feel. I need to show someone that I'm good at something. I can throw tight spirals and sometimes catch bullets. I can dribble between my legs. I know a trick softball pitch.

Randy has something called an M-80, an unusually thick firecracker, some fraction of the potency of a stick of dynamite, though exactly what fraction cannot be agreed upon. The idea seems to be to put the M-80 in a glass Coke bottle on a cement brick in the fuzzy green conduit they call *the creek*, then ignite it. There's no way the fun can ever measure up to the hype.

Shortly before or shortly after the big bang, I begin to study the sky. As the boys investigate the powder and the black stain on the concrete, I think even if I were to run to Uncle Jim's house and phone my mother, even if she were home and willing to make the rescue trip immediately, we are still miles and hours apart. There is the highway and all that highway sky between us.

Guerneville, CA, Spring 2000 –

Clare can't take time from work, nor does it feel fair for me to ask. We traveled to Baltimore as a family only five months ago. It's been more than a year since I went to see her folks in Wisconsin. But I need to go home. *Home*. And I feel I need to take Lucy, our five-year-old California blond, the delight of her grand-mother's heart. I want Lucy to know her grandmother because my mother is so often in my thoughts as I help to raise Lucy. Lucy needs to know the source of my best bedtime songs and my slow wonder at her, or is it my need?

Baltimore, MD, Spring 2000 –

My mother looks much thinner and frailer since our last visit: amyotrophic lateral sclerosis, aka Lou Gehrig's. She hasn't the strength to use the walker any-more, not even to cross from sofa to dining room table. Her legs are as sturdy as boiled pasta. Now my father hoists her from bed to wheelchair to stair-lift to wheelchair to sofa, etc. I do much of the lifting and pushing on this visit, a chance for him to rest. At night, it is the same routine in reverse. Sofa to chair to stair-lift to chair to bed. Some days she does not come downstairs at all. She says she's not in pain, but she gets frustrated, especially in bed when her arm gets trapped behind her back.

On the first day of our visit she is alert and engaged. She draws Lucy out on kindergarten, the incorrigibility of little boys, the surprising wisdom of our cats. She admires each of Lucy's crayon creations, has me tape them to her bedroom door. She directs me to boxes in the back of cabinets where colorful coins, feath-ers, beads, and scarves have been tucked away. One box has dozens of hand-carved animals, my favorites when I was a boy. Lucy spreads out the menagerie on the carpet.

On day two, my mother frequently needs the oxygen tube. I use the suction to clear mucus from her trachea. I squirt saline through the plastic cannula, clean the rim with a Q-tip. She's too exhausted to talk. Lucy sits beside her on the sofa, sucking her thumb and twirling her Grandma's hair in her fingers.

So go days three, four, and five: sad, boring, sad, helpless. It's a ten-day visit. We spend hours on the sofa watching cartoons or Regis and Kathie Lee and many more hours at the bedside. Conversation is sparse and always difficult, punctuated by coughing and the rattling of the suction pump. I have the feeling I should be feeling other than how I feel – an all-consuming hatred for Regis Philbin, terrible restlessness. Lucy and I take walks around the neighborhood. I point to houses with special memories.

"Mark Vincent lived there," I say. "He knew all the pressure points. He could give a mean charley horse. And that's where Pat Rogers lived. He was mentally retarded."

"What's that?"

"He was slow. Like his thinking was slow."

"Like he would talk real slow?"

"No, like he would stand on our back porch and tell us to go home."

"How can you go home if you are at home?"

"Exactly."

Poplar Drive, Larchmont, West Park – I show Lucy the field where we played football, the alley where we played kick-the-can, the cemetery where we climbed on mausoleums, the pharmacy in Woodlawn where we'd sit on chrome-rimmed stools and sip malteds. The sky, the trees, the houses are so different from those in her little town in California. At first, it seems Lucy is excited by the differences, but lately she seems drawn to anything familiar. After we share a milkshake, day six, Lucy says the words I am dreading: "I miss Mommy. When can we go home?"

Homesickness attacks the lungs first, a sudden, surprising labor of breath, dead weight in the solar plexus. It spreads outward and upward from the center, fills one's head like the exhaust from a bus. Distraction is the only pill, and with repeated doses it has diminished effect.

"We'll see Mommy soon," I say, but I know that four days to a five-year-old is not soon. *Soon* means nothing. "We're going to New York to see a friend, to ride on the train, to go up in the big eye-scraper." (Lucy's word) "And then we'll return to visit more with Grandma, and then *then*, we'll get on the plane to see Mommy."

This habit of plotting the hours and the days, this ongoing litany of activities, becomes a sickness all its own.

NYC, Winter 1986 –

But I did love Pia, even if I couldn't project my feelings into the future. I was on the brink of twenty-four, and everything seemed forever and impossible. Marry me, marry me, marry me: in a moment it was as much love as I had ever felt.

"Have you ever been in love, Milton Mittelman?"

"You're nuts, mister."

"Did you ever feel so lonely it hurt to breathe?"

"So many questions," he says. "Who do you think you are, Perry Mason?" He smiles. He's pleased with his joke.

"How's the sandwich?" I ask.

"I'm having lunch with Perry Mason."

"Then you must be Paul Drake," I say.

"Oh, a real comedian," he says. His corned beef on Russian rye looks enormous in his hands. I watch it begin to slide apart after the first bite. I ought to quit my questions and let him eat or we'll be here all day; but I am Perry Mason, and the investigation has just begun.

"I was in love," I say, "but I didn't believe we'd be happy together. Does that make sense?"

He puts down his sandwich and picks up his slice of pickle.

"I broke it off."

"That one?" he asks.

"Yes, Pia. She's come by the workshop many times. She kissed you once."

"You should marry her."

"I couldn't do it."

Milton shows me the rotating finger. Crazy.

"Now," I say, "love seems like something else, smaller. It's like I've made it so, and I can't go back."

Rotating pickle.

"You must have been in love, Milton. Sometime?" As soon as the words come out, I think maybe not. Maybe he's never been in love. I wish I hadn't said it.

He bats his eyes. "I love *delisandwich*," he says. I laugh, and he shrugs, a turtle-ish look, a smile. And then with less conviction, he says, "My mother, sometimes."

"How do you know when you love her?"

"Here we go again," he says.

"It's the last question. I promise."

"You promise?"

I put my hand on my chest where my heart should be. He seems unimpressed.

"Yes," I say. "Yes, I promise."

"When I miss her."

Trenton, Summer 1973 –

Michael needs to make some phone calls and pack his gear for the night. He doesn't know if he'll be able to get a sleeping bag for me. Maybe there will be fishing in the morning – somewhere not far away where Michael insists the trickling green conduit turns into a rushing river full of bass. I take my place on the front stoop under the big New Jersey sky. I miss my friends, my brother, my sisters, my father; but when I look at the gray clouds, scarlet streaks, it is my mother who feels so many deep breaths away.

Camping, it has been agreed, will be in Randy's backyard. The day had been overcast and the night is starless. Randy has a lantern. Michael has a half pack of cigarettes. J.T. snatched a half pint of blackberry brandy from his father's cabinet, and Jeff has a box of Ritz crackers. I have nothing to share. Michael proposes we have a séance, and the proposal is met with a chorus of "Fucking A." We make a circle of our bags (in my case a pair of blankets), and we lie, elbows propped in wet grass, facing the lantern.

J.T. tells an aimless tale about the life of Houdini, though he gives much greater attention to Houdini's death. There's disagreement regarding what happened to the body, who saw it last, etc. When the blinking red lights of an airplane pass overhead, it is unanimous – That was a sign! Houdini heard us calling him!

Michael tells the story of Bloody Mary. It is the night of her prom.

"I'll bet she was a fox," says Randy.

"No, man." Michael has everyone's full attention. He's in his element. "She was a ugly bitch." He toys with the wick of the lantern, pretends as if she's heard what he said and flared up in anger.

"You're a crazy motherfucker," says Randy.

"The guy that took her to the prom was just doing it to have some fun. And to get her off his back because she was telling all the other bitches that he liked her and shit. He never took her to the prom. He got all dressed up, and she was like all dressed in this long white prom dress, and they got in his car, but he took her up some steep curvy road by the ocean."

"It must've been California," J.T. suggests.

"It's just a fucking story," says Jeff.

"Bullshit!" Michael pounds his fist in the grass. "It happened." Then, after a brief quiet, he says, "Yeah, it was California. That's what it said in the paper."

"I don't believe this shit," says Jeff.

"I don't really know if I want to hear this," I say.

"Pussies," Randy says.

"It's cool," Michael says. "But you can't be here. You'll ruin it."

So I gather my blankets, and Jeff rises to his knees but then he reconsiders. "Fuck it," he says, and he's back in.

"You have to leave," Michael tells me.

"Go back to Baltimore," says Randy.

"At least go around the side of the house," says Michael, "else we won't get a sign."

"No," I say, "I guess I'll stay." My loneliness is more pointed now than ever, sharper than my fear.

"You can't stay," Michael says. "You can't."

I am, though I hadn't realized it until this moment, committed to the idea that someone far away can hear our pleas. Why can't this group of boys invoke the spirit of Bloody Mary if my mother feels my desperation? I find a place to sit in the carport, my back against the house. I can hear Michael very clearly when he begins again.

"So he drives her up this road, and she says, 'Where're we going?' but he doesn't say anything. Then he pulls over. Then he kisses her. Then he tells her to get out of the car because he wants to look at the ocean. And she says, 'But I'm scared.' And he says, 'Don't be scared with me because I'm in love with you.' And he walks her right up to the edge of the cliff and goes like he's about to kiss her again and says, 'Die bitch,' then gives her a push."

"Yeah, I've heard this story," says Jeff.

"Shut up, man," Michael says.

"Shut up or I'll kick your ass," Randy says.

"And she crashes on the rocks way down below," Michael says. "And the guy just stands there for a minute. He's looking over the edge to see if he can see her, and what he sees is the whole ocean turn blood red."

"Holy shit. Did you see the flame when he said that?" J.T. says.

"He's fucking with it," Jeff says.

"I'm not fucking touching it, man."

"If you're out there, give us a sign, Bloody Mary."

"Give us a omen," says Randy.

"Give us a sign, any sign."

NYC, Spring 2000 –

So maybe this'll be fun. Maybe Lucy will find a way to shake her sad, heavy feeling. A trip to NYC has done it for me a few times. From Penn Station we walk directly to the Empire State Building. Lucy seems impressed, but not like I'd hoped. She's intrigued by the elevator. At the top she's most interested in the coin-operated binoculars, tilts them back, and looks at the big, gray sky. She asks, "When can we go home?"

We take a subway to the East Village in search of a deli I'd told her about; a place which holds some special memories for me, but it's gone, or I haven't re-membered the right street. We settle for slices of extra cheese pizza at Ray's – the best pizza in the world, I tell her. She pulls cheese off the top, and after two bites she can't eat anymore.

We meet Pia, as planned. She's married and has a boy two years older than

Lucy. I haven't seen her in eight years, but one drunken night several months ago, I called her. It was a whim, perhaps, or some felt need to bridge my past and present. I don't know why I did it. I was home alone with a pint of whiskey, and I thought I might hang up when I heard her voice. We talked. As it happened, she'd lost her father less than a year ago. She'd said she wanted to call me but didn't know how. We marveled at our wish to reconnect with our former lives and particularly with each other. Conversation was fast and easy, then strangely quiet and difficult. We exchanged email addresses. As far as Clare knew, Pia was just a friend, a former co-worker.

It feels easy. It feels safe. It feels very safe when I see Pia has put on thirty pounds since I last saw her. We'll just be friends. Lucy shows a surprising burst of energy when she meets Pia's boy, a bookish little Phillip with wire-rimmed glasses, a charming speech impediment, and a funny, embarrassed smile. Thunderclap: Lucy hasn't had a playmate the entire trip! The kids slurp paper cups of gelato and climb on the statues in front of the courthouse. Lucy likes to climb. She's braver and more agile than he is. Her sudden happiness feels odd, like she's punch-drunk or like she's suffering that *Parents Magazine* dread Clare warned about: overtiredness. Lucy pretends she needs to kiss Phillip and when he blushes and dodges her, she giggles too loud, too long. It's as if she's doing a commercial for FUN.

I've worn her out, I think. This trip to NYC was for me, not her. My mother is dying, and I'm in a frantic search for home, any and all of the places I've grown up. I haven't quite let go of the image of young Pia, nor of the possibility that we might rekindle something, find a quiet place to fuck. I hate myself. We walk over the Brooklyn Bridge, the hum and rattle of traffic beneath us. Pia and I stab at conversation, but I keep turning to check on Lucy. I need to see her face because when I can't, her laughter sounds like crying.

Trenton, Summer 1973 –

Again I can't eat dinner. Emotions are involved, some complication when it comes to swallowing. I can't make a good apology. I try to conjure up the kind of boy who could handle this situation while Aunt Jan looks meaningfully at Uncle Jim and passes a plate of not-fully-cooked perch dressed in last night's stewed tomatoes. Jim doesn't meet Jan's eyes. In fact, I never see them communicate at all. He rinses his plate and is off to his Jim world – fast horses, cold glasses of beer, pipe smoke, or so I imagine. Jan rinses her plate and tells me there is a bag of plums in the refrigerator. She tells Michael to stay out of trouble and then reminds us that Stacy will be home in two hours, so we should save her some dinner. She searches her handbag, smoothes on lipstick, and she's gone.

Michael gives me a shrug on his way out the front door. I feel a shudder inside, a wince in my heart. *Pussy.* I fail. But there is another feeling rising in me like the bubbles in the glass of Aunt Jan's Tab I've poured for myself. I pull a knob on the TV and see a thin white line flicker and spread into a dark grainy picture. The channel numbers here are not what I'm used to – another tiny dart of homesickness – but all I can find is New Jersey local news anyway. As I watch the screen, I devour plums, nine of them, each one an adventure of sweet, soft flesh, pink, pale purple and some the color of wet sand. A firefighter is carrying a child from a brick tenement as smoke curls out from blackened windows. I turn the channel and see the same firefighter talking with a reporter and wiping sweat from his forehead. And on the next an animated lemon is crying sparkling tears into an animated candy disc. I'm bloated and bored, but somewhere in the dark my resolve is building. I will tell Jan or Jim, the next one I see, to call my mother. I WANT TO GO HOME. So what if Randy/Michael think I'm a pussy. They're only part of *this* world. Their fun isn't fun. They suck.

NYC, Winter 1986 –

"Milton," I say, "you know why we've come out to lunch today, right?"

He looks up but he doesn't speak. His sandwich finally slides out of his hands. The remaining bread, corned beef and mustard look like they were sliced on the subway tracks. I notice that the rain has washed both sides of his glasses clean, and I'd grown so used to the dust and dried flecks of skin collected on the inner rim. My little Down's syndrome friend with the ill-fitting dentures and the sebum-spotted spectacles, your tryingly limited repertoire of comebacks: "You've always been my favorite." As time funnels, he becomes all the clients I've known and cared for; this deli becomes the city I love.

"I'm moving to California. Today is my last day of work."

He swallows and says, "They have earthquakes there."

"I wanted to tell you I'll miss you." And I've always felt your dignity, *or is it your indignation?* I raise my water glass and say, "So many times I've felt proud of you."

"What do I say?" he says.

"I don't know what's to say."

He looks at his plate and puts his hands in his lap. "I had a feeling."

"How? Why?"

"Perry Mason again."

"How did you know?"

"Because the other one took me out to lunch."

"Your bench-work supervisor before me."

He nods.

"What was her name?"

He shrugs.

Easy come, easy go, right? What was I really hoping for? I don't know. "Do you want some rice pudding?" I ask. "I think it's in the budget."

He makes his eyes big and silly. "No one ever bought me rice pudding before."

Brooklyn, Spring 2000 –

We've crossed the bridge, and my suitcase has grown heavier, Lucy's hysterics more hysterical, Pia's boy Phillip apparently irritable. He doesn't want to be kissed or chased. Lucy doesn't want my hand cupped under her chin or my attention at all. We agree to take a taxi the rest of the way to their brownstone.

I seldom took taxis when I lived in NYC, and I rode the subway only when necessary. I worked on West 13th Street, and I lived in an apartment on Broadway at 125th. Three or four days a week I'd walk home from work past the big brick apartment houses of Chelsea: rolling racks of furs and fabrics in the mid-thirties; black suits and yellow taxis swarming like bees in front of Penn Station; gallon-sized, plastic vats of spices in Hell's Kitchen; destitute men and women camping on cardboard mattresses outside the Port Authority Bus Terminal (what the seasons do to unprotected skin); blinking neon GIRLS GIRLS GIRLS of Times' Square (everyone wanted to put a flyer in my hand, but I was too fast); the chaotic grid at Columbus Circle spilling into the cool, quiet grandeur of Lincoln Center; pastel bright yuppie buzz at 72nd Street and on up, past baby-joggers, fitness centers; exotic groceries, sidewalk cafes with glamorous waiters in black and white; the new and not so new Chinese, Japanese and Thai eateries with bunted banners announcing Grand Opening; overflowing bookstores, boxes of paperbacks out to the curb; bars; students; Greek diners; more students; the stone and wrought-iron significance of Columbia, Barnhard, The Manhattan School of Music; Union Theological; the homeless, everywhere homeless; the spare-changers; the woman who always needed money for Pampers; the long shadows of the Morningside Heights projects beneath which the median widens, tracks emerge, and the subway seems to rise to meet the elevated platform. Often I was lonely, but never bored.

On weekends I'd walk half the length of Manhattan to the East Village to sit in Thompkins Square Park or on a stoop on Avenue A and watch the army of Doc Martens, plaid trousers and leather, spiked hair and shaved heads, safety pins, sunglasses, faces, faces, faces. I'd walk until I had to rest and then sit as if on a beach or boardwalk to watch the surf roll in. NYC had the best waves I'd ever seen.

Sometimes I'd walk east on 125th into the heart of Harlem to smell incense burning and see posters of Martin, Malcolm, Marcus, Nelson, the African headdress, little black girls in white lace coming from church, liquor stores with triple-thick glass, the great Apollo Theater, the Cotton Club. I absorbed the aromas of fried chicken, cornbread, sandwiches Cubano, and sweet potato pies, and marveled at the stones of the buildings, the glistening tar of the streets – that I could be a part of it just by being there.

At first I'd felt dwarfed by The City, and frightened, and I needed in some perverse way to throw myself at it. After a second mugging, a brutal one calling for seven stitches in my upper lip, I felt even more determined, an even greater need to mark the streets as mine. I believed whoever I'd become, I'd become him here. Homes: battlegrounds, mirrors, oppressive and awesome. Homes are settings, of course, but characters, too, arch enemies, buddies, foils, lovers, foiled loves.

Pia's husband is a fashion photographer. He's in Toronto. I've never met him. Her Phillip brightens after the cab ride. He invites Lucy up to his room to see his collection of rubber dinosaurs. Pia pulls out an icy bottle of Absolut and two glasses from the cupboard. She leads me to a little plot of garden in the back. It's peaceful now away from the noise and heat of cars, even better after the first cold sip.

"How's Derek?" I ask. "How's everything?"

She grimaces. "He has his interests, and I have mine." She seems uncomfortable with this, and I can see the face inside her face, feel a flood of memory, bad times. "He's a good father," she adds.

"Are you happy with Derek?" I give her a searching look. I don't know what it looks like, but I think it says, *I can make you feel better.* She excuses herself to get more ice.

What the fuck am I doing?

Trenton, Summer 1973 –

I didn't hear Stacy enter the house, and I don't know how I could have missed her. She appears at the foot of the stairs in her nightgown and looks at me on the sofa in the living room, but she shows no sign of recognition. I'm worried she might have heard me talking to myself. I think I said "pussy" a half dozen times, and I said, "Fuck Randymichael."

She says, "Did you eat all those plums?" She's barefoot, and she's working her thick brown hair into a high pony. I hear the refrigerator door open and close. "I can't believe it," she says.

I can't wait to go.

"Where's little rat face?" she says.

"Michael?"

"Who else?"

"I don't know."

She stands in front of the TV. "He just left you here?"

"Yeah, I guess." She's still gathering her hair in a fist and with her arms above her head the hem of her nightgown dances up to the tops of her thighs and beyond. Her panties are so tight or pulled so high that they show the precise shape of her vulva. I see the curled fringes of her pubic bush, and I see that she sees me looking. She stops toying with the pony and turns her back to me, changes the channel and the volume to her liking.

"He must be out with Randy," she says. "That asshole."

"I guess," I say, but I'm not sure which one she's calling asshole. She moves only slightly out of my path to the television, and she begins a series of stretches. Head to left knee, then to the right, half split, full split, backward arch; my god. I feel the plum pulp moving in my belly, a twisting and tightening in my Fruit of the Looms, and a painful constriction in my throat. In her upside down position, she cranes her neck slowly right and then left and again she catches me before I can shift my gaze back to the set, and again she gestures toward modesty by lowering her hips to the floor and pulling down on her hem. I think I ought to get a glass of water, do something, but I'm too embarrassed to stand, sure that the shape of my shorts will reveal me. She eyes me as she pedals her invisible bicycle; then she kicks her legs over and touches her toes on the floor behind her. Her panties are buried deep in the crack of her ass, and as hard as I try, I can't look away.

Enter Michael through the front door. He greets me with a non-look and offers a few unkind words for his sister. Suddenly the show is over, but still I can't stand up.

It's the morning of the next day when I find Uncle Jim filling his pipe at the counter between kitchen and dining room. "I think I want to go home," I say.

He nods or twitches, I'm uncertain; but then he looks utterly confused.

Aunt Jan comes around the corner drying her hands in a towel, her brows furrowed. "What's the matter, sweetie?"

"I just want to go home."

"You're not having a good time," she says with a lilt that surprises me.

Should I protect her feelings or be honest? I shrug.

"Are you sure?" She looks at Uncle Jim.

I nod.

"Michael will be so disappointed."

I try to imagine this. I nod.

She looks long at Uncle Jim, and he bites the air. It never occurred to me they might say no. Do I need to make an exhibition of my misery? I'm thinking as fast as any eleven-year-old ever has when Uncle Jim says, "Can you ride the train by yourself?"

"Yes!"

"Are you really sure?" Aunt Jan asks. "Really, really sure?"

"Yes, yes, really yes."

Brooklyn/NYC, Spring 2000 –

Pia takes twenty minutes getting her ice. Maybe, I think, she's putting in her diaphragm? Jesus! I pour more vodka and then some more. "Just cut it out," I say to myself. "Just masturbate," I say, as Pia passes through the door.

"What?" she says.

"Where did you go?"

"Your daughter is upstairs crying. She didn't want to tell me what's wrong."

"Oh shit, really?"

Pia's face fills with worry—for me, I think. I stand too fast and send the picnic bench hard onto the bricks behind me. When I bend to set it upright, I feel the vodka full force. I feel all the years that have passed, dizzy and ridiculous. "Where is she?"

"She's upstairs."

"Oh, you said that."

I stop at the foot of the backstairs beside Pia and give her forearm a squeeze. I mean to say, "Thank you" and "I'm sorry" and "Please don't worry about me" and "I'm a good father."

Lucy is standing in the hall on the second floor.

"Honey?"

She's not crying anymore. The grime of the city has made her cheeks slightly darker, and her tears have cleaned two pink stripes.

"What's wrong, sweetie?"

Her shoulders are hunched, and she turns half away from me, almost facing the wall.

"Can you tell me about it?"

She shakes her head.

"Do you want to come and sit with me?"

She doesn't answer but permits me to take her hand. I lead her down the stairs.

We pause for Pia on her way up. "Time to put Phillip to bed," she says. "I'm exhausted."

I nod.

"Guess you're tired, too."

I nod again and try to smile.

"I put a blanket and sheet on the sofa bed," she says.

Morning. "We'll take the subway to Manhattan and then the Amtrak to Baltimore and then ..." The full litany again, this sickness, this adulthood. "Hey," I say to Lucy, "are you okay?"

"I'm hungry," she says.

"I know where we can get the best breakfast in the world."

"My feet hurt, too, Daddy."

"We won't walk too much, I promise."

We say our good-byes, fast and awkward, and Lucy and I head out, hand in hand down Flatbush Avenue. Jackhammer, hydraulic tamper, the painful scrape of a backhoe pushing a steel plate over a hole, dust, exhaust, mounds of garbage heaped at the curbside; I forgot how bad the city can stink on a hot day. And now I remember a friend from Guerneville who said, "You can't smell your own house, not unless you've been away for awhile." He was talking diaper pail, cigarettes, mold under the drain board. He was struggling for a word: *assimilate, assimilitize, acclimate, acclimatize*. He's a chimney sweep, a rough-edged, backwoods, knucklehead philosopher. Like a number of people I've met in that community, he knows a whole lot, especially about how things work and how they break. He's Lyle. I've thought about him plenty on this ten-day venture into single parenthood. For almost as long as I've known Lyle he's been battling his ex for a fifty-fifty split of Molly, their daughter. Molly happens to be Lucy's favorite playmate. Lyle and Molly – another story, perhaps.

On the subway, Lucy sits, and I stand in front of her. I squat to look in her eyes. "What happened last night?"

"I don't know." She shrugs and looks away. I look around the car to see who might be listening. It's crowded, but it seems everyone is hiding. All the faces make me tired.

"You can tell me," I say.

"He wanted to touch my private area." She tilts her head toward her lap, in case, I guess, I don't understand.

"Why didn't you come and get me?"

She shrugs. Her cheeks slacken. "I didn't know where you were."

"Did he touch you?"

"Sort of."

"Sort of?"

"With dinosaurs."

"Oh, Lucy. Were you scared?"

She shakes her head, then a little nod for yes.

"Sweetie." I look at her face for a long time, three station stops, then under the river into Manhattan. Finally she lifts her gaze to take in her fellow passengers. She seems embarrassed but suddenly not so far away. I stand and take hold of the overhead rail. The man beside Lucy is staring out the opposite window of the train, eyes oscillating rapidly, reptilian or machine-like, I'm not sure. I wonder if he's thinking or dreaming now. I wonder if there's a pocket in his brain that will hold this fleeting moment.

Baltimore, Summer 1973 –

It's drizzling outside the station in Trenton. Uncle Jim walks me to the ticket counter, then the platform. He digs out his pipe from the pocket of his raincoat. He's busy with pinching, packing, and the tilt of his flame. No sloppy good-byes here.

I love my seat. The first clicks and clacks of motion are distinct and countable, and I wonder how many between me and home, but then they come faster like the rain as we chug south. Pinpoint drops glide across the glass and converge, swell into mini-puddles, quivering reunions.

My mother, as it turns out, is not quite so big as the sky. She looks very small seated between two broad-shouldered, big-breasted black women on the platform bench. She wears a clear plastic rain bonnet and holds a lavender silk scarf on her lap. She doesn't see me, and the thirty feet from the train door to her bench feels longer for the pounding on the corrugated tin roof above the station. I tread toward her slowly, my suitcase an inch above the ground. I stay wide of her peripheral vision because I'm a scientist, and I'm measuring the shape of my heart. I'm bouncing sonar off the ocean floor, the deepest, darkest part. I'm Joe Mannix, private investigator. I'm Paul Drake retrieving evidence for Perry Mason. Will she feel me? Will she turn and see me just by my thinking it? Give me a sign, any sign.

She turns! She smiles! She cups my face in her hands, cool and wet, and kisses me below the eyes, alternating left and right, one, two, three, and she pulls back to look me up and down and then again kisses one, two, three. "You must be hungry," she says.

I nod.

"I know a deli nearby."

"Okay," I manage, though I can't hear my own voice.

"Do you still like matzo ball soup?"

"Yes."

"Of course you do. It's perfect on a day like this."

Guerneville, 2000 – Another Story –

We're on a beach of the Russian River. Lucy and Molly swim the thin channel, about fifty feet across, to a woodsy peninsula with a narrow silt bar. They're finding river clams, as small as a child's thumbnail, and placing them in a muddy pool. I dig into my backpack past mangoes, sourdough bread and sunscreen to find a pint of Jim Beam. Lyle has some white powder to share. These are good times, moving toward excellent… or maybe not.

"You want to hear some shit?" Lyle asks.

Lucy's blond and Molly's dark brown hair both look golden in the late afternoon sun; little girls with little shoulders and boyish hips running tiptoe in the shallow water.

Lyle and I sit in the shade of a twisted laurel and some tall reeds of fennel. I feel the burn and the drip and the rush from a line of Lyle's speed. I chase it with a shot of J.B. and then a swig of water from a plastic 7-Up bottle.

"Whew boy, that's nice!"

"This might not last," Lyle says. He's got the sad brown eyes and jutting chin of Bruce Springsteen but not the gravitas, or not usually.

"What 'this'?"

"Megan's taking me to Family Court. She wants full custody."

"That's bullshit," I say. "Molly would die if she couldn't be with you."

He takes a swig. "I think I'd die," he says. He looks at his feet in the muddy sand. "I want to run away with her."

"Don't do it. Megan's just freaking out again. You've been through this before."

"Well, you've got to fight for what you love," he says. He slips the whiskey back into my pack. "But Megan's got the upper hand this round."

"What does she have?" I ask, but as I say it, I realize she might well have a dozen things. Like what if she knew what we're doing right now? She'd flip. So would Clare. So would all the cops and judges of Sonoma County. Megan would scream if she saw the girls on their bikes without helmets or if she saw them wrestling over a paddle in the canoe. She'd go nuts if she saw Molly and Lucy riding in the bed of Lyle's pickup on West Side Road. And sure, there's plenty of good cause for worry, but her world is haunted by nitrites, pesticides, poison ivy and sleeper waves, and I think – and *I feel* – life's too fucking short – only two days a week for Lyle – to always play safe, to pass up corndogs and blue popsicles and rollercoaster shrieks and to worry, worry, worry about getting to bed on time.

I can see that Lyle is thinking – does he want to tell it straight or tell a story? My mind flashes to something Clare said she saw in a magazine, an article for women whose men are turning forty. She listed the symptoms – no big surprises – the usual shit: sports cars, reckless investments, affairs, hair implants, almost none of which hold any appeal for me. *Almost, ugh!* We laughed, Clare and I. She congratulated me on having what the magazine called healthy self-esteem, solid values. I said it's because I'm not bored with my career – because I never fucking had one. I laughed. I wasn't freaked about turning forty, not yet.

"She's got a photo," Lyle finally says. We're sitting now. He's smoothing down the hair on his shins. He lights up a Swisher Sweet, and I light my hand-rolled Drum.

"Of that?" I tilt my head toward the bag with the compact mirror and straw.

"Nooo, not that." He chuckles. "Remember," he says, "the time I bargained for an extra day and took Molly up to Shasta?"

"Your ski trip. Molly had a great time." But I'm not saying anything; Molly always has a great time with Lyle. Lucy, too. When the four of us get together we have wild adventures; every hour is fully packed with minutes. Swinging on the rope swing over the river, climbing rocks at the coast, snatching three-pound crabs from the oily water under the marina in Bodega Bay, scaling four fences and a very steep hill to inspect the mudslide in Rio Nido; the time we snuck into the pumpkin patch with the corn maze at midnight.

"You forgot sunscreen, right? Molly got a little burn on her face?"

"Yeah," Lyle says, "but that's not the worst of it." He shakes his head. "Listen," he says, I'm like a fucking spider. Or a monkey. I'm a fucking spider monkey in a cage. I'm doing upside down push-ups on the ceiling. That's me."

"All right," I say. "You're restless. I know that."

"No, man, I don't sleep. Sometimes I think my heart wants to explode out of my chest."

"Maybe you need to cool out on the powder."

"It's just maintenance," he says, "but maybe, maybe you're right. Anyway, that's not the fucking point. Do you want to hear this?"

"Yes."

"It's not *my* heart."

"Now you've lost me."

"Listen," he says, "Do you know how a two-stroke engine works?"

"I told you, I don't know how anything works."

"Never mind. Listen."

"I'm listening."

"I still love Megan. I do, even though I can't stand her. I love her. I daydream all the time about how things were. And it eats Molly up, too. That's why she gets like she does."

"Yeah, I know."

"Like all that rivalry bullshit, like sometimes she's just got to get her way over the stupidest, stupid anything." He lets out a heavy sigh. "It's because she's scared."

"Lucy gets like that."

"Not the same."

"No."

"The two people who taught her what love is stopped loving each other, or at least that's what it looks like to her."

"And so you or Megan might stop loving her, or that's what it could look like?"

"But I don't ever want her to think that, ever. You know? Because I don't feel that, ever."

"That means you're under a lot of pressure."

"Aren't we all?" he says. "We all are."

"So tell me about the photo."

"But I want you to understand how stupid I can be. But it's not just stupid, it's, well, very stupid."

Lucy calls out, "Daddy look! We found forty hundred clams!"

"Yeah, Daddy, get over here and look!" Molly hollers. And to Lucy, "It's not forty hundred!"

Lyle says, "It's a picture of her left hand. Her hand is white and the rest of her is pink. There's not much to see, really, but there's a doctor's report, too. She got frost nip." He mutters something I can't hear. "I mean, shit, she's fine now, but it's just more ammunition for Megan to take to court."

"Didn't Molly have gloves?"

"Come *on*, Daddy!" Molly yells.

Lyle and I stand and walk into the river.

"She wanted to try the big slope," he says. "With me. She wanted to hold my hand. Skin on skin, you know? Do you know what I mean?"

We're dog paddling, eyes and noses an inch above the water. I can see the light bouncing off the river and rippling up the steep bank on the opposite side. It feels like the hazy film of a dream. The girls are standing on the silt bar now, hands on their knees. "Come *on*, Daddy!" Molly screams. "You've got to see," says Lucy. The closer we get, the less it seems they can contain their excitement. They break into bunny hops and clapping, and they even hug each other. They run to inspect their pool of clams, and they run back in time to take our hands and guide us out of the water. "Come on, Daddy. Come on. Come on."

"I think I know what you mean," I say to Lyle.

"No," he says, "You'd know if you knew. You'll know."

Baltimore, Spring 2000 –

Baltimore has a Penn Station, too. Pop is waiting there for us. "Hi, Pop," I whisper. We don't hug because Lucy is asleep in my arms. Her thumb is in her mouth, and one of her fingers tangled in my hair. I spread her out on the backseat. The chest of my t-shirt is moist from her saliva and warm from our sweat. I feel suddenly cold, empty, relieved, not relieved. My father puts our bag in the trunk. "Thanks," I say. "Thanks for coming down to get us. Who's with Mom?"

"The hospice nurse came around noon," he says. "Then Sylvia. And Angie came over as I was leaving."

"Wow," I say, "a full house."

"Your poor mother. It wears her out." His voice is quiet and soft, but his walk from trunk to driver's seat looks brittle, and I remember my mother having used the same words, *Your poor father. It wears him out,* as we watched him carrying her lunch tray into the kitchen, halfway across the carpet before he could straighten to his full height.

"It must be hard for Mom to talk when she can hardly breathe," I say.

"Yes," he says, and then, "You look exhausted."

"You, too."

He shrugs. He can't be exhausted; there's no time for it. He's a thoughtful man, but on the subject of his feelings or his needs, he speaks in simple platitudes. Lately he's fond of, "One day at a time." It's as if he thinks his feelings don't deserve deeper consideration or that he just plain doesn't want it. His days are plotted around the activities which sustain my mother: soaking and cleaning of respirator tubes, morning suction, replacement of the cannula, replacement of the bandage, awkward tango from bed to chair, cleaning of dentures, dressing, blood sugar test, insulin shot, preparation of a balanced breakfast, mid-morning suction, pre-lunch suction, lunch, dishes, afternoon suction, shopping (MWF), dinner prep, second fistful of pills, dinner, cozy up on the sofa with Jim Lehrer, empty and rinse toilet bucket (on one of her good days), bedtime reading, removal of dentures and cleaning, undressing, third fistful of pills, evening suction, awkward dance from chair to bed, careful arrangement of pillows, final blood sugar test, transition onto the respirator (too much here to attempt to describe), goodnight kiss. For all his efforts, she's losing weight, losing muscle and losing coordination. He's put on a few pounds around the middle. He lumbers up the stairs, head down with one handing pulling the banister. He naps once or twice a day. He enjoys the New York Times crossword when he can.

"How about a bite?" he asks. "Maybe Lucy would fancy a real Baltimore crab cake?"

"I think Lucy wants a bed."

He nods, but I wonder if he's a little disappointed. This would have been an opportunity for him to get out and do something different. On my last few visits, after my mother was plugged into the respirator and we'd had our goodnight kisses, my father and I stayed up late, shared a few beers and talked. It'd become the time to catch up on each other's lives and trade impressions of my two sisters and brother who also live in California, who have also made frequent trips back to Baltimore to offer help. Invariably we'd consider the progression of the illness and what the future might look like. There'd be long periods of silence, and these felt important. I'd hoped to talk with him more this visit, but Lucy never adjusted to the east coast clock. She was up till midnight every night, and she needed my attention. He would have liked to take us down to Washington's Natural History Museum and watch an IMAX special or even simply to feed the ducks together at Woodlawn Pond, but I was set on showing Lucy NYC, and of course, visiting Pia. I know I'm selfish and, ironically, I want to be alone so I can think less about it. I search my tired brain for a joke. He likes jokes. His laughter is explosive and wonderful.

"So," he says, "Milton Berle was visiting a senior center. Have you heard this one?"

"No," I say, but I think I have.

"He made the rounds, shook hands with the old men and kissed the old women. Then he found a little old woman sitting by herself, and he said, "Excuse me, ma'am. Do you know who I am?" And the woman said, "No, but go up to the front desk, I'm sure there's someone who can tell you." My father laughs loud enough to cause Lucy to stir. If my mother were here she'd make a crack about people who laugh at their own jokes, and he'd start in again, harder and louder.

My mother has a deadpan delivery like Jack Benny or Bob Newhart. It seems even drier now with the extra beat for her to put her finger on her trach tube before speaking. Before we enter the house, I can hear Sylvia, my mother's former co-worker and best friend, talking in her breathless voice. It's a good sign. It means my mother had the strength to make the journey down from the bedroom to the living room. She'll be very tired. I wonder if Sylvia poured her a finger or two of her Manhattan mix. It tends to help.

Sylvia greets Lucy with enthusiasm, but Lucy looks drunk with tiredness. She can barely lift her head off my hip. Picture five characters: 1) Stage right is an elderly gentleman, kind but socially uneasy. He ravages his pockets and comes up with the hard currency of purpose; his keys and wallet to place on a shelf. He makes awkward greetings, and it is painfully obvious he's eager to pass through the room as quickly as possible. 2) Stage center, standing like a conductor is Sylvia with red capillary cheeks. She is grace and ebullience, but she's picked a hard crowd to entertain. She is performer and audience, a performing audience, a swell of hyperboles that makes our blood retreat in embarrassment. She nearly embraces, then pulls back from, 3) Lucy, leaning into stage center, unwitting and unwilling, one side of her face pink and slightly swollen from sleep, cheek matted from the coarse car upholstery, hair pressed flat, eyes narrow from sleep and what looks like suspicion. 4) Me. I'm not sure what I look like, but my smile feels raw and tight like it does with cologne after a dull shave. I feel trapped with Lucy leaning on me or hiding behind me and Sylvia standing one-and-a-half electric feet away, but my attention is pulled to stage left. 5) My mother sitting in the corner of the sofa, her blue stocking feet propped on an ottoman, a pair of clear plastic tubes draped over her bone thin calves and swirled in the lap of her blue and lavender housecoat. One of her hands rests on a cushion and the other is poised near her throat in preparation for speech. Her eyes are bright and wet, slightly magnified by her glasses. She seems to be drinking Lucy in, her face, her entire presence – my mother's expression is a mix of delight and anticipation. I look down at the face pressed to my hip. Is there any reciprocation here?

Grandma to Lucy, more animated than usual: "I'll bet you had an exciting time in the Big Apple."

Lucy to me with a look approximating scorn: "When can we go home?"

Me to Lucy: "Can you give Grandma a kiss?"

Lucy presses her face harder into my shirt.

Me to my mother, unspoken: *She loves you. She's tired.*

My mother to me, unspoken: *I'm a lot tougher than you think, mister.*

Grandma to Lucy, softly: "I'm sure you're missing your mother."

Sylvia: "You've been away a long time for a little girl. You'll be flying home tomorrow, right?"

"The day after," I say.

I'm about to launch into a new litany when my mother says, "Maybe you should give Clare a call." And to Lucy, "Do you think you'd like to talk to your mother on the phone?"

I've made this suggestion at least five times, and Lucy has steadfastly refused. At the mention of Clare, Lucy has always turned sullen, so I've avoided mentioning her. I think I understand how that works, like it is better not to read the menu if you are broke, but the analogy has limitations, e.g. when you are hungry you don't typically feel resentful toward food, and you don't likely fear that food has stopped needing you. At this point, I don't understand any better about how a two-stroke engine works, but I think I get it; on some visceral level I understand that my heart is not simply mine, not mine alone.

"Clare will be at work now, California time. I'll call her later," I say. "You can talk to her if you want to sweetie, but you know you don't have to."

"Maybe it will make your mother too sad," my mother says with two long beats for Bob Newhart and one more for the trach tube. "Your poor mom. She probably thinks you've forgotten all about her."

At this Lucy pulls her face out of my shirt and cautions a glance at her grandmother. At first it looks as if she's squinting into bright sunshine, then her face softens. I don't know if I want to cry or clap. "Have you ever seen Sponge Bob Squarepants?" Lucy asks. She offers me a tentative smile and skips three steps across the carpet to kneel beside my mother on the sofa. She kisses her Grandma on the cheek. "I have a video in my backpack," she says.

Spring 2001 –

I made a solo visit to Baltimore on April 11 and returned to Guerneville on April 21, a day before my fortieth birthday. Thirty minutes after I reached my living room my father called to say, "Mom died." His words were simple, but I heard deep sympathy in his tone. He had been a lawyer most of his life, and it is like him to present the facts. "She suffocated at 12:15, about four hours after you left for your flight. She'd been having more than usual difficulty moving air in and out of her lungs, and the oxygen from the nasal aperture was insufficient, so I tried to put her back on the night respirator. That's when I lost her. We did."

He told me he was sad, but that he'd be okay. He said he thought she was tired of fighting the illness. He thought she was ready, and it was a relief she died quickly and painlessly and at home. We all knew she dreaded having to go back into the hospital.

Suffocation is frequently the cause of death with A.L.S. Death can come very slowly, slow enough for other basic body functions to shut down, slow enough to make one feel threatened with the loss of the last thing she has – her dignity. Sadness, sadness and relief.

One Last Unforgivable Digression – April 20, Baltimore

On the last night in my parents' home, we had a very close call. My father was sleeping, and I was doing the bedtime routine. I'd done it a few times before, and I felt confident. In fact, I wanted a sterling performance – a shining memory.

During the ten-day visit I'd brought homework with me. I'd been reading and ranking stories for a literary magazine I'd started with a couple of writer friends. I was fiction editor. My career, ha ha. (This *is* another story). I'd read thirty or more out loud to my mother, and I'd found her to be a very helpful critic. We enjoyed comparing impressions. Perhaps because ours was an SF based magazine, we received an inordinate number of gay love stories, some of which had triple-X features.

On this last night, the last story we read together offered some graphic depictions of rimming and fisting. I paused mid-way through the second locker room scene to ask if she'd like me not to continue. She sipped water from her flexi-straw and said, "I think we should finish it." And just before I started reading again, she said with music in her voice, "The varieties of human pleasure." (For what it is worth, only the sex scenes were rendered carefully; the rest of the story was a toss-off. On our one-to-ten scale, I gave it a two, and she gave it a three.)

I had wanted to read her my only "10" in the fat stack of manuscripts, a bizarre futuristic piece about a city of Kens and Barbies and dog-people, not my style at all, but every line sparkled. It ended with a beautiful surprise that at least briefly renewed my faith in the power of words to convey complex feelings. She was too tired, though, and I had to tell myself I'd get another chance.

I gave special attention to flattening the sheet beneath her, arranging the air cushion best to protect her sore backside. I ran the suction pump five times and rinsed the cannula twice in distilled water. I rubbed her feet with aloe vera cream. I helped her down just right, almost.

The last step in the process was to connect her trach tube to the respirator. Before the hook up, I inflated a thin plastic cuff in her throat, which is necessary to form a tight seal but also makes it impossible for her to speak. Each night the inflation of the cuff feels final, and at the end of each visit absolutely morbid – *these will be the last words I hear from her.* Before I pressed air from the plastic hypodermic into the plastic catheter, she told me it was hard to breathe, even though we'd done a thorough suctioning. She said emotions make her throat swell – giving a very literal meaning to the expression "choked up." She said she was tired and that I looked tired and that she loved me – twice she said she loved me – and she reminded me that I was named after her father, whom I'd never met, but who, she said, was the kindest man she'd ever known. Her eyes brimmed, and she smiled her denture-less smile and said, "You're a kinder critic of stories when you've had a glass of whiskey," and then she gave the signal with her hand that meant for me to inflate the cuff.

About one minute after we made the transition onto the mechanical breathing device, she indicated with a hand at her throat that it did not feel right. I asked her if she wanted me to unhook it and start the process over and she turned her head left and right to say no. I asked if emotions were making it hard to breathe and she blinked yes. We waited. She closed her eyes. And then, perhaps half a minute later, she opened her eyes and indicated difficulty again, her hand shaking at her throat. I unhooked the respirator, and she could not regain her breath. I screamed for my father. He appeared promptly, looking groggy and startlingly frail in his BVDs. We quickly discovered that the tank downstairs was connected to the nasal aperture and had not been re-connected to the night respirator. She had not been getting any air. She passed out. Her eyes rolled up to eleven o'clock, and her cheeks became slack and cool to the touch. My father administered emergency oxygen with a hand pump and a mask as I leapt down the stairs and connected the tubes as they should have been.

It was two or maybe three minutes before her eyes rolled back down, approximating a look of consciousness. Another minute passed before she gave any sign she recognized my father or me. She wasn't able to say anything about what she'd seen or felt, except that she'd heard me screaming, "Come back." She told us she had not felt me pinching or slapping her cheeks, but she had felt the cool wet cloth I put on her forehead. And she said, "I was lost. It was dark, but I wasn't scared. I never felt alone."

Clare, Lucy and I; my brother Brian, his wife Kay, and their children Hank and Melanie; my sister Vicky and my sister Anne – nine in all, six adults and three children – gather together at Vicky's apartment in San Francisco. The funeral will be in Baltimore one month hence, and my father has discouraged any of us from flying out sooner, given the cost, given our immediate obligations, and perhaps, though he doesn't say it, he prefers the privacy now. We have each had phone conversations and traded emails with him, but his absence is surely felt. So, of course, is hers. We gather to *remember* her. It seems too soon to say it, but also not.

Our ceremony goes like this: each person takes a turn saying something she or he remembers about Mom (Grandma for the benefit of the children). With each spoken memory, we light a candle in the center of the room, and then after a moment's quiet, extinguish it. We are not a religious family, and so I think, the ritual, any ritual, makes us a little self-conscious. As a symbolic gesture, blowing out the candle feels odd, more like forgetting than remembering, thin curls of black smoke dissipating before our eyes, but the kids like it immediately, and it seems to make it easier for everyone to speak.

Anne: "I remember how Mom used to hit the gas and shriek when we came to the rise on Flannery Lane – how she could make something so ordinary so fun."

Vicky: "I remember the feeling of her hand on my forehead when I was sick. It felt good to be sick."

Lucy (blushing): "She always has nice surprises. I like to twirl her hair."

Me: "These came from Dad's email: I liked the way she said, 'Thank you,' how gracious she was in her illness. And I remember her face that said, 'Don't take yourself so seriously.'"

Brian: "I see her all the time in the expressions of Hank and Melanie. Hank has her sweet tooth. Melanie has her look of mock indignation."

Kay: "I admired her independence and the way she was never afraid to speak the truth. I'm going to miss her so much."

Clare: "She was a wonderful grandmother. She made me feel like a good parent."

Hank: "I remember when we went to New York. She bought me a little Statue of Liberty."

Melanie: "She would always tickle my back real soft. It felt nice."

Anne: "It felt like a gift to be able to help her."

Me: "It seemed like she could tell me who I am."

Vicky (laughing): "That was good or bad?"

Me (laughing, too): "Both, of course. I'll miss it."

Brian (imitating Mom's voice): "I've been onto you since the day you were born."

Vicky (singing one of Mom's favorite songs): "Is you is or is you ain't my baby."

Anne: "It doesn't really seem real."

Lucy: "I want to go see her. I think Mommy could make her better."

Melanie: "I don't think you understand, Lucy."

Kay (soberly and kind): "It's a mystery. It is for all of us."

It's a mystery for all of us, even beyond the ken of Perry Mason. I mean, what happens when people die? I mean, where did *she* go?

I've been collecting evidence for almost thirty years, but I don't know how to interpret it. Back now in California, I bike over to Lyle's. "Okay, Lyle," I say, "I think I know why you had to hold Molly's hand, skin on skin. Not I think. I know. Tell me the other part."

"You want a beer?"

"What else you got?"

"Vodka in the freezer. Where's Lucy?"

"Clare took her to see the bat lady at the library. She's got real bats. And puppets, too, of course."

"That's cool."

"Way cool."

"You don't like bats?"

"No, I do…"

"You've got to check out bats sometime. Their wings are like our hands, five bones, five fingers. I've been thinking a lot about bats."

"I was hoping you could tell me about the two-stroke engine."

"A thing of beauty," he says, "very efficient, but not without problems."

"Oh?"

"They burn up oil and make filthy exhaust."

"What's so cool about them?"

"It's their power-to-weight ratio. You get twice the power in the same space because there are twice as many power strokes per revolution."

"So instead of intake, compression, combustion and, um–"

"Exhaust, right, that's right. Here you have only two strokes, compression and combustion. With every revolution the spark plug fires."

"Hmmm."

"It's like your heart when you're in love."

"Hmmm?"

"Nothing is wasted. Putting out and taking in; it's all part of one simple cycle – it feeds itself."

"This is helpful."

He illustrates by pumping one fist in a rhythmic gyration. His elbow, I think, is a piston. "Think of the power stroke," he says.

"Thanks, Lyle." I raise my shot glass and down my vodka. I set the glass on the railing of his deck and straddle my bike.

"This is what happens if you don't maintain fluid levels." He grabs his chest and falls back against the side of his house.

"I see." We laugh.

"You off?"
"Yeah. I told Clare I'd meet her after the bats."

Lucy has a play date, and Clare and I have a sex date.

Pedaling, it's a push and pull cycle, past the river in soft morning light; long, green, gentle ripples – this is home – the breeze that bends the tops of the tall pines; the way the leaves turn their yellow sides up; the way the scotch broom breathes in and out, ecstatic like a child laughing, like a bodybuilder pulling into his full flex; the orange, white and gold poppies bobbling on their frail necks. And on I push into dark cool shadows and out again into sunlight, puffs of tiny life blowing across River Road. I am home, and I am headed home, not to Baltimore or NYC with their memories and their particular challenges. This is Guerneville, land of the Russian River and big-ass, beautiful redwoods. I picture Clare putting paper bats into a manila folder or spraying Shout on a stained jumper at the bathroom sink or paying bills at her desk – nice pictures. I imagine her folding down the sheet, setting the plastic jar of Astroglide within easy reach.

I pedal faster.

Everywhere –

I'm still unclear about the two-stroke engine. Giving is taking is giving. It's powerful and efficient but also noisy and messy? It seems something like an idea of love. When I say my heart is not mine, not mine alone, evidence abounds. I think of music, the sky, the largest living organism, a mycelium twenty thousand acres wide. I think of oceans and the smell and the sound of rain and of the big and small sacrifices people make every day.

But when I feel in terrible doubt – after losing my mother, after turning forty, after searching and despairing for signs of who I am – it helps to remember my homesickness and the night in Baltimore when I phoned Clare and asked Lucy to say hi to her mom. My father and mother had already finished their nighttime routine and gone to sleep. Lucy and I were in the basement – what had been my father's office until my mother's illness confined her to an upstairs bedroom and tethered him to the reach of her weakening voice. The rooms down below were lit by a single unshaded lamp, and we became accustomed to stepping over stacks of books, papers, coils of extension cords to the inflatable mattress which was our bed.

"Come here, Lucy," I said. She backed away from the phone but finally permitted me to hold the receiver to her ear.

"Hi, Mom," she managed and then fell silent.

"Mommy can't hear you nodding," I said, though I suspected Clare could.

"Okay, okay, yes, Mom, I know," Lucy said. With the tips of her teeth she kept her lower lip from shriveling.

When my turn came again, I told Clare I loved her and missed her and we'd see her very soon. Then I hung up and searched for Lucy. She had slipped behind a paneled partition, crouching in the shadows. She'd tucked her chin between her knees, and her tears were rolling over her cheeks and spilling onto the floor. She was quivering. I hugged her and gave her the litany, but very short this time. We held hands on our way up the stairs to the kitchen, where we shared cookies and glasses of milk. When we finished, we descended to our bed. I clicked off the light. I wrapped my arms around her and squeezed, my chest pressed to her back. Shortly, I could feel her breathing settle into its somnolent rhythm, but I couldn't sleep and wouldn't dare. The proof, Perry Mason, was suddenly so palpable. Two hearts. One pulse.

www.ingramcontent.com/pod-product-compliance
Lightning Source LLC
Chambersburg PA
CBHW050916120626
46552CB00004B/1599